GRANGER SCHOOL
AGAWAM, MASSACHUSETTS

Manufactured in the United States of America

Library of Congress Cataloging in Publication Data

Ishinabe, Fusako.
  Hiro's pillow.

  Translation of: Ohirune ippai.
  Summary: A little Japanese boy napping on his pillow
is joined by various woodland animals.
  [1. Naps (Sleep) — Fiction.   2. Sleep — Fiction.
3. Animals — Fiction.   4. Stories in rhyme]   I. Title.
PZ8.3.I784Hi   1989   [E]   89-11768
ISBN 0-944483-44-5

HIRO'S PILLOW

Fusako Ishinabe

 **GARRETT EDUCATIONAL CORPORATION**

Here is a boy you'd
like to know

Who lives in Japan.

His mother sews
all his clothes
And even makes
pillows when
she can.

A backpack, a
   red hat,

Socks, a school bag
   with a car —

These are just some
   of the things
   that
His mother has
   sewn so far.

The little boy — Hiro is his name —
Likes to sit and watch his mom
Rather than play a game.

"Here's something new that I made
     for you,"
Hiro's mother said one day.
And it was a wonderful surprise —
A Teddy Bear pillow with large
     button eyes.

"Come on, Moko, let's go outside,"
Said Hiro to his dog.
"I want all my friends to see
What my mother has made for me."

They run to the meadow and
look around,
But nowhere is a friend to
be found.

"There's no one here
  in the meadow,
There's no place
  else to go"
So Hiro puts the
  Teddy Bear down,
And he and Moko
  lay on the ground.

Soon in the grass so green and deep,
Both Hiro and Moko fall fast asleep.

A little bear comes walking past
And sees Hiro and Moko in the grass,
Sleeping so soundly that they
    cannot hear
The little bear who is so near.

The little bear sees Hiro's pillow
And quickly runs to his home.
Now he's rushing through the meadow,
Carrying a pillow of his own.

He quietly puts it down
And falls asleep on the ground.

Soon other animals come
dancing around
The three who are sleeping
on the ground
They all run home, as fast
as they can go,
To get their own favorite
pillow.

Back they come, on the run,
With pillows of all sizes and shapes.
Red ones, brown ones, yellow ones, too,
There's a pillow of almost every hue.

Then Hiro gives a yawn
And slowly looks around.

He can't believe what he sees
Lying next to him on the ground.

The little bear is sound asleep,
Clutching tightly to his pillow.

And all around all over the ground
Are other animals sleeping in the
meadow.

What a surprise for Hiro to see
Animals asleep on pillows — just like
you and me!